ROT

12X12
31/

This

The
a fu

To Ewan, Jenna and Charlotte with love – T.K.

For Ramshackle Rosie, Hornswaggle Harvey and Aye Aye Ava,

for Pirate Polly and Cap'n Kristina – A.G.

Bloomsbury Publishing, London, Oxford, New York, New Delhi and Sydney

First published in Great Britain in 2017 by Bloomsbury Publishing Plc
50 Bedford Square, London WC1B 3DP

www.bloomsbury.com

BLOOMSBURY is a registered trademark of Bloomsbury Publishing Plc

Text copyright © Timothy Knapman 2017
Illustrations copyright © Ada Grey 2017

A CIP catalogue record of this book is available from the British Library

ISBN 978 1 4088 4938 5 (HB)
ISBN 978 1 4088 4939 2 (PB)
ISBN 978 1 4088 4937 8 (eBook)

All papers used by Bloomsbury Publishing are natural, recyclable products made
from wood grown in well managed forests. The manufacturing processes
conform to the environmental regulations of the country of origin

Printed in China by Leo Paper Products, Heshan, Guangdong

1 3 5 7 9 10 8 6 4 2

Timothy Knapman

Ada Grey

ROCKABYE PIRATE

BLOOMSBURY

LONDON OXFORD NEW YORK NEW DELHI SYDNEY

Rockabye Pirate, in the crow's nest,
Mummy says bedtime, and Mummy knows best.

You've had your adventures,
you've sailed the high seas,

so under the covers
and go to sleep, please.

The sharks and sea monsters you chased through the day

are tucked up in bed now, and snoring away.

The wickedest pirates who ever set sail,
Black-Bearded Brewster, Sea Dog McPhail,
Cross-Eyed Delaney and Freddy the Fright,
have tied up their ships and gone home for the night.

While the skies up above are all spangled with stars there'll be no more **yo-ho-ing**, and no more **a-haarrs!**

They've eaten their suppers, cleaned teeth and - my gosh! -

they've **jumped** in the bath and they've had a good wash.

And when it was time, amid **wails** and **boohoos**,

those **bloodthirsty pirates**
have had their **shampoos!**

Cutlass, eyepatch and peg legs hung up on a hook,
they huddle around Mummy and her big storybook.

All day they struck fear
as they stood on their decks

and turned other ships
into jibbering wrecks.

But now they kiss teddy,
while a lullaby hums,

and snuggle down deep, and start sucking their thumbs.

Under Jolly Roger duvets they dream pirate dreams
about wild pirate parties – with pirate ice creams! –

where everyone's naughty, and no one says **"thanks"**, and they all get a chance to try walking the planks.

Then they sail in their dream boats to impossible lands
where a chest full of treasure hides under the sands.

And it's easy to find it,
and snaffle the lot,

if you've got an old map
where **X** marks
the spot.

But adventure can wait now,
and pirating's ceased
till the lookout spies morning
in the skies to the east.

There's scarcely a ripple
on the face of the deep . . .

And Rockabye Pirate has fallen asleep.